The Enormous Turnip

Retold by Vera Southgate M.A., B.COM
with illustrations by Mélanie Florian

LADYBIRD 🐞 TALES

ONCE UPON A TIME in the spring, an old man sowed some rows of turnip seeds in his garden.

As time went by, the rain fell on the seeds and the sun shone down on them and the turnips began to grow.

Every day, the turnips grew a little bigger. But one of them grew much faster than all the others. It grew large, then very large, then huge, until at last it was enormous! No one had ever seen such an enormous turnip.

One day, the old man fancied a plateful of turnip for his dinner. He took off his jacket, put on his big boots and went out into his garden.

He gathered up the leaves of the enormous turnip in his two hands, in the proper way, and he pulled.

He pulled and pulled with all his might, but he could not pull up the enormous turnip.

So the old man called to his wife
to come and help to pull up the
enormous turnip.

The old woman put her arms around
her husband's waist.

Then the old man pulled and the old woman pulled.

They pulled and pulled with all their might, but they could not pull up the enormous turnip.

So the old woman called to a little boy to come and help to pull up the enormous turnip.

The little boy took hold of the old woman's waist.

Then the old man pulled and the old woman pulled and the little boy pulled.

They pulled and pulled with all their might, but they could not pull up the enormous turnip.

So the little boy called to a little girl to come and help to pull up the enormous turnip.

The little girl took hold of the little boy's jumper.

Then the old man pulled and the old
woman pulled and the little
boy pulled and the little girl pulled.

They pulled and pulled with all their
might, but they could not
pull up the enormous turnip.

So the little girl called to a big dog to come and help to pull up the enormous turnip.

The big dog took hold of the little girl's belt.

Then the old man pulled and the old
woman pulled and the little boy pulled
and the little girl pulled and the big
dog pulled.

They pulled and pulled with all their
might, but they could not
pull up the enormous turnip.

So the big dog called to a black
cat to come and help to pull up the
enormous turnip.

The black cat took hold of the big
dog's tail.

Then the old man pulled and the old woman pulled and the little boy pulled and the little girl pulled and the big dog pulled and the black cat pulled.

They pulled and pulled with all their might, but they could not pull up the enormous turnip.

The black cat called to a tiny mouse
to come and help to pull up the
enormous turnip.

The tiny mouse took hold of the black
cat's tail.

Then the old man pulled and the old woman pulled and the little boy pulled and the little girl pulled and the big dog pulled and the black cat pulled and the tiny mouse pulled.

They pulled and pulled with all their might.

And this time they did pull up the enormous turnip!

It came up with such a jerk that they all fell down flat on their backs.

The enormous turnip fell on top of the old man.

The old man fell on top of the old woman.

The old woman fell on top of the little boy.

The little boy fell on top of the little girl.

The little girl fell on top of the big dog.

The big dog fell on top of the black cat.

The black cat fell on top of the tiny mouse.

After a moment, they all jumped up, shook themselves and started to laugh. They laughed and laughed for a long, long time.

Then they carried the enormous turnip into the old woman's kitchen. The old woman cut up the turnip and cooked it for dinner.

Then the old man and the old woman and the little boy and the little girl and the big dog and the black cat and the tiny mouse all had turnip for dinner.

They all ate and ate until they were full. But they could not eat all of the enormous turnip.

There was plenty of it left for dinner the next day and the day after.

And that was the end of the enormous turnip.

A History of
The Enormous Turnip

The tale of *The Enormous Turnip*
is still a very popular story today.
It is one of several lyrical stories that are
often called 'cumulative' or 'chain' tales.
The story relies on repetition
and rhythmic text to progress, with
a new character adding something
new to the story. The pattern of words
combine to create a rhythm that is
a little like a tongue-twister.

The Enormous Turnip or *Giant
Turnip* was first published in 1863
in the collection *Russian Folk Tales*
by Alexander Afanasayev. This original
version of the story included much
of the same rhythm and rhyme that
can be found in the tale today.

Ladybird's classic 1970 retelling by
Vera Southgate has brought the tale
to a new generation and helped to
keep it a firm favourite today.

Collect more fantastic

LADYBIRD 🐞 TALES

Cinderella

Hansel
and Gretel

Little Red
Riding Hood

The Three
Little Pigs

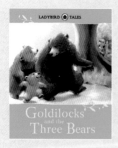

Goldilocks
and the
Three Bears

The
Gingerbread
Man

Snow White
and the
Seven Dwarfs

Rapunzel

Rumpelstiltskin

Sleeping
Beauty

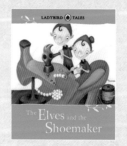

The Elves and the
Shoemaker

Puss in Boots